Recipe
For a Story

Ella Burfoot

Macmillan
Children's Books

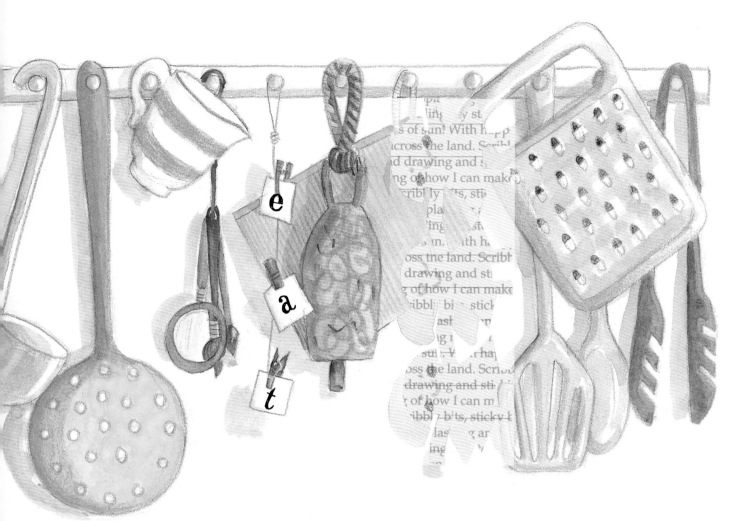

I am going to cook a book!

I'll break some thoughts into a cup.

I'll beat them, whisk them, mix them up.

I'll weigh out the words – just enough.

BIG WORDS

small words

MIXED WORDS

Choosing the right ones can be tough!

The small ones go into the pot,

HE, SHE, IT, WHEN

and

WHAT.

I'll drop some big words from a height,

ELEPHANT,

CROCODILE,

DYNAMITE!

COOKING FOR CREATIV

AWFUL AUTHORS AND TERRIB

Fairy Cakes and

TASTY TAL

WOLF IT DOWN by B.B

GOLDILOCK

FANTASY
FLANS   and

The Princess ar

EC
Y CA

Now that my story has begun,

I'll cut out characters, one by one.

Feelings, colours, sounds, a picture
All add flavour to my mixture!

Giggly Word Preserve

ZAP MA
WO

Sad Words

I'll add a watery word or two.

I'll pour them in and stir them through.

Splish, splosh, splash, drip or sprinkle.

Glug and gurgle, squelch and tinkle.

Now I'll put a lid on it.

Wait a while.

Let it sit.

It's not until I roll it out

That I'll find out what it's all about!

And now I'll lay it in the tin,

So
my
characters
can
jump
in!

Next, the middle,
　　the action, the filling!
Into the pan,
　　without any spilling.

Now all I'll do
　　is simply add
A spoon of good
　　and a pinch of bad.

Turn up the heat -
　　let the bubbles quicken.
And then my plot
　　begins to thicken.

MONSTER FLAKES

Alphabet Spaghetti

BITTER BEANS

BOWS and FRILLS

SWEET PEAS

Granny's

WOLF

Weet

SLICES OF QUINCE

Full Stop   Capital Lett

Dried
Princess Peas

Every sentence
   will taste much better
If I add a full stop
   and a capital letter.
But where did I put them?
   I've seen them myself . . .
Here they are in the cupboard,
   on the top shelf!

STORY POPS

Porridge
Oats

ENORMOUS
TURNIP
Slices

Lastly the ending - I'll press it down,
And add decoration all around.

I will glaze with happiness,
leave it to cook,

Then bake it, brown it,
and finish my book!

I turn the pages and I can tell

That my recipe's turned out well.

I've done everything that I need . . .

To make my story a delicious read!